TO ALL THE TEACHERS AND LIBRARIANS
WHO HELP US LEARN THE *RIGHT* WORDS TO SAY
—A. K.

TO THE FUZZY BROTHERS
—D. C.

Margaret K. McElderry Books · An imprint of Simon & Schuster Children's Publishing Division · 1230 Avenue of the Americas, New York, New York 10020
Text copyright © 2007 by Alan Katz · Illustrations copyright © 2007 by David Catrow · All rights reserved, including the right of reproduction in whole or in part in any form. · Book design by Sonia Chaghatzbanian · The text for this book is set in Lomba. · The illustrations for this book are rendered in watercolor and colored pencil. · Manufactured in China · 10 9 8 7 6 5 4 3 2 · Library of Congress Cataloging-in-Publication Data · Katz, Alan. · Don't say that word! / Alan Katz ; illustrated by David Catrow.—1st ed. · p. cm. · Summary: Michael's rhyming description of his day at school has his mother repeatedly interrupting to prevent him from saying impolite words. · ISBN-13: 978-0-689-86971-6 · ISBN-10: 0-689-86971-1 · [1. Etiquette—Fiction. 2. Schools—Fiction. 3. Stories in rhyme.] I. Title: Do not say that word!. · II. Catrow, David, ill. III. Title. · PZ8.3.K1275Don 2007 · [E]—dc22 · 2006000686

DON'T SAY THAT WORD!

written by
Alan Katz

Illustrated by
David Catrow

MARGARET K. McELDERRY BOOKS NEW YORK LONDON TORONTO SYDNEY

*What happened
in school today, Michael?*

A lot!
Listen to this!

Rebecca brought in birthday cookies—
oatmeal, fudge, raisin, and sugar.
Lee gave the whole class the ookies—
he picked and topped his with a . . .

At recess we all saw a spider
and a bird that went chittery-chirp.
Doug snorted as he drank his cider,
then let out a two-minute . . .

DON'T
SAY
THAT
WORD!

We laughed and Ms. Grant wasn't happy.
She threatened to punish the group.
As she called, "Go in, make it snappy!"
she stepped in a pile of dog . . .

Some kids played a mean trick on Jesse—
with their gum they did you-know-what.
His chair was all gummy and messy,
and suddenly so was his . . .

Next we cleaned our cubbies together,
and Max found his mom's favorite scarf.
But he'd better hope for warm weather—
while holding it, Max had to . . .

DON'T SAY THAT WORD!

Max bawled, Mom, and you should've seen it—
the scarf, he really did soil it.
Things got worse when Liz tried to clean it
by flushing it right down the . . .

In Art my pal Richie got inky.
But Mom, that was only the start.
'Cause Richie then made the room stinky
by blasting a really big . . .

"Well, Michael . . .

Today was a sea of great dramas.
I hope there are calm days ahead.
Run along—put on your pajamas.
It's late and you should be in . . .

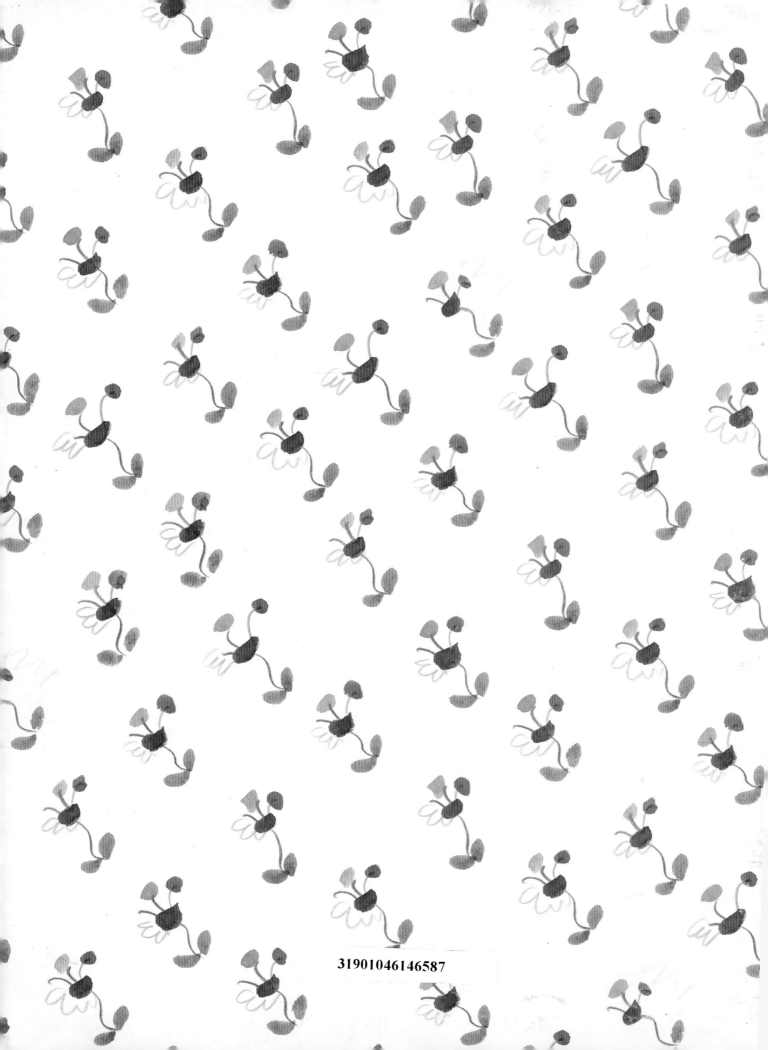